I GOT YOU YOU BABE

PAUL COCCIA

ORCA BOOK PUBLISHERS

Published in Canada and the United States in 2023 by Orca Book Publishers.
orcabook.com

Library and Archives Canada Cataloguing in Publication
Title: I got you babe / Paul Coccia.
Names: Coccia, Paul, author.
Series: Orca currents.
Description: Series statement: Orca currents
Identifiers: Canadiana (print) 20220185239 | Canadiana (ebook) 2022018531X |
ISBN 9781459834705 (softcover) | ISBN 9781459834712 (PDF) |
ISBN 9781459834729 (EPUB)
classification: LCC PS8605.O243 I2 2023 | DDC jC813/.6—dc23

Library of Congress Control Number: 2022934493

Summary: In this high-interest accessible novel for middle readers,
Mac wants to do a duet with Amy for the school fun fair.

Orca Book Publishers is committed to reducing the consumption of
nonrenewable resources in the production of our books. We make
every effort to use materials that support a sustainable future.

Orca Book Publishers gratefully acknowledges the support for its publishing
programs provided by the following agencies: the Government of Canada,
the Canada Council for the Arts and the Province of British Columbia
through the BC Arts Council and the Book Publishing Tax Credit.

Edited by Tanya Trafford
Design by Ella Collier
Cover artwork by Getty Images/Massonstock
Author photo by Shirley Coccia

Printed and bound in Canada.

26 25 24 23 • 1 2 3 4

To Matthew and Amanda,

for a Sonny and Cher talent show routine

that is the stuff of legend, and to Vesna, for her

inspiring adoration of the Goddess of Pop

Chapter One

"The Fun Fair is always so boring," I say.

"Mac Riley!" Dad warns. "Mind your manners. We're discussing new business. We're not bashing the Fun Fair." He is head of our school's parent association and chair of this meeting. A few of us students have been invited to provide input for the Fun Fair committee. Which is totally what I'm doing.

I hear Chandra and Jenny snicker. The biggest jerks in our grade. One of them whispers loud enough for me to hear, "Why is Mac always so much drama?"

I roll my eyes. I turn my head a little to give them what I hope is a threatening look. The girls lean into each other and giggle.

Amy elbows me and whispers, "Don't pay any attention to them. Eyes on the prize, Mac."

My best friend is right. I can't forget our plan. We have to do this properly. I'm not exaggerating— the Fun Fair is a total snooze, not at all the big community event it could be. Every year it's the same old thing. There's a sad bouncy castle, a water-gun fight and some face painting. We get some families with little kids in the area, but most of the people who come are students from our school. And they show up to hang out with their friends. But I have an idea that could change everything.

I stand up. "This *is* new business," I say. "The Fun Fair is not only a community event but also our biggest fundraiser of the year. But I think everyone can agree that it's become pretty boring over the past few years. It's time for something new. Something flashy. A real draw."

"What do you have in mind?" Dad asks, sighing. He takes off his glasses and rubs his eyes.

"Well, since you asked," I say with a grin, "I've got an idea. Something to give the Fun Fair a little glitter. And a whole lot of sparkle." I walk around the room and hand everyone our information package.

I had wanted to use playful fonts and print the handout on flashy paper. Amy said we'd be taken more seriously if we used plain white paper and black ink. More professional, she said. I don't know. I think it looks so boring. Kind of like the Fun Fair. So I made up for it with my outfit. I'm wearing black skinny jeans and an oversized sweatshirt with sequin roses that change color depending how you stroke them. I totally caught Chandra and Jenny eyeing it with envy when I walked in.

"What is this?" Mrs. Khatri, the treasurer, taps the piece of paper. "A Pride Carnival? I need to know more."

"It's a makeover," I say. "Making the Fun Fair a Pride-themed event not only breathes new life into it but also makes it clear that everyone is welcome and included and wanted." Amy helped me with that wording. She said being cool wasn't a strong enough argument and that we should try to sound more adult.

"While I hear what you're saying, Mac, I'm not sure adding a theme to the Fun Fair is the way to go," Dad says. "The fair already brings in a good chunk of money every year. We don't want to mess with what works."

I nod. I knew he'd say that. "But what worked before isn't working now. If you compare the reports from the last few years, you'll see the Fun Fair isn't doing as well as it used to. That's not good." I pause for effect, then pick my next words to sound as grown up as possible. "My partner with the proposal, Amy Chen, will now join me."

Amy jumps to her feet and rushes over to the easel at the side of the room. She's wearing skinny jeans and a floral T-shirt under her hoodie. I chose her outfit so we'd match. She places two huge pieces of poster board on the stand.

"This graph," Amy says as I position my hands like I'm revealing a prize on a game show, "shows a steady drop in profits over the last five years. And if the trend continues, this year's Fun Fair will only make half as much as it did in its top-earning year."

"All this information is right in the package in front of you," I add.

Amy removes the first piece of poster board from the easel.

"These graphs," she says, as I point theatrically to the second board, "show how much money Pride events around the world make. Of course we're not expecting this type of result from a school fair. But it does prove that people want this type of event. And they're willing to pay for it. Included in your package is a news story about a school in Australia that held a Mardi Gras Pride Fair. They made a lot more money than they had in previous years."

Mrs. Khatri leans forward in her seat. "How much more are we talking?"

"Over 30 percent," I say. "That's a pretty big increase."

The parents turn to one another. They begin to chatter.

Dad hushes everyone. "I can see you've done a lot of work," he says. "Very impressive for two twelve-year-olds. We'll review your ideas and think about it."

"But the fair is coming up soon," I say. "If you don't decide tonight to go ahead with this new idea, it won't happen. At least, not until next year. It's now or never, Dad. Decision time. Avengers assemble!"

"Bit much," Amy whispers. "Take it down a level."

Mrs. Khatri looks up from the handout. She stands and walks over to our chart. She leans back a little as she reads through it. "These numbers are promising. The kids are right. There won't be time to prepare if we don't decide tonight. This could be *just* what we need to raise some more money. We should call a vote."

My dad puts his glasses back on. Then he flips through our package. Reading more slowly this time.

"Come on, Dad," I say. "Please? We did this right. We collected all the facts and data. We brought it to the meeting. Amy even made me choose a serious font to print it in. Nothing with swirls."

"Such a diva," I hear someone say. I assume it's Jenny. Whatever. "Diva" isn't even an insult. Definitely not when you are one. And I so am.

"Okay," Dad finally says. "Any other thoughts before we go to a vote? Anyone?"

No one speaks at first.

Then Mrs. Khatri says, "Just one worry. Not everyone likes…sparkle. Some people may not support the event."

"Are you saying you're not in favor?" Dad asks.

"No, this is a great idea," she replies. "But I think we should be prepared for some pushback. I hope there isn't any. But we should be ready."

"We want to make this a safe and positive event. Is the risk worth it?" Dad asks.

"It's a gamble. But think of what we could do with the extra money we bring in. For the school. For the students. For our kids. Things we've had to say no to because we didn't have the means, we can reconsider. I vote we turn this year's Fun Fair into a Pride Carnival."

"Raise your hands if you agree," Dad says to the group.

Almost everyone raises their hands. Jenny and Chandra slouch in their seats, arms and legs crossed. No raised hands from them.

"Charles Middle School will hold its first-ever Pride Carnival," Dad announces. "Thank you, Amy and Mac."

Amy high-fives me.

I give her a huge hug.

"We did it! Carnival time!" I cheer, lifting her off her feet.

"I told you the professional font was the way to go."

Chapter Two

"The bouncy castle has to have rainbow stripes," I say. "And one of those really tall slides. We can get strobe lights. And have a dunk tank. And multicolor cotton candy. And fireworks. Oh, and the talent show! The winner could be declared Grand Marshal of the Fair. No. That's for a parade. How about Sparkling Crown of the Carnival? Now that's got a nice ring to it."

I'm sitting behind my dad in his car. Amy is buckled in across from me.

"And I'm going to be the Sparkling Crown!" I finish.

"*If* you win," Amy says.

"When. Not if. Don't I deserve to win? This was all my idea. Who else would be a better Sparkling Crown? No one."

"Slow down, Mac," Dad says as he comes to a stop light. "You've got a lot of big ideas. But we do have a budget."

"A lot of *good* ideas. Plus, the talent show won't cost anything," I argue. "We have that portable stage we use for gym assemblies. We can set it up outside. Near the baseball diamond. We can hook up some lights and speakers."

"The talent show is fine. It's all the other things you're talking about. Renting some of those things isn't going to be cheap," Dad says.

"Cheap is not the look we're going for. We want

it to look like a happy cloud exploded in joy. Cheap is gross. Never say that again to me," I say.

My dad gives me a look in the rearview mirror. I know not to push it further.

Amy giggles quietly though. I smile at her.

Since Amy and I met on our very first day of school, she has always been there for me. When I told her I wanted to have a Pride Carnival, she was the one who helped me. We did the research together. We made the charts and graphs together. We planned what we'd say together. She was the one who had the idea to dig through all the previous years of meeting minutes to get the funding information for the charts. She knew how to find the stats on Pride events around the world. She has the brains for that kind of stuff.

"Your dad has a point," she says. "Your taste isn't cheap."

I glare at her and try to give her the "don't push it" look my dad gave me in the rearview mirror.

"Don't you use your angry eyes on me, Mac Riley. They don't work. Everything you're suggesting sounds fantastic. *If* they can figure out how to pay for it. This was our idea, and they went for it. We need to be realistic about what can be done."

"You mean my idea," I correct her. "I thought of it. Remember?"

Amy reaches across the car and shoves me gently. "You wouldn't dare let me forget. Not even for a second. But *we* got the committee to agree. And you know what I'm saying makes sense."

My dad chuckles. He's been hearing the two of us banter like this for years. Going back and forth. Discussing and arguing. But always best friends. In fact, part of what I like best about Amy is she gives it back. I mean, she gets I'm a diva. She gets that that's a good thing too. Not like Chandra and Jenny. But Amy doesn't always let me get away with everything. I'd never tell her, but I need that. I need her. She keeps me real. She really does get me.

"The parent association will handle things with the vendors," Dad says. "That's not really a job for you two."

"We still need to help," Amy insists.

"With posters and prizes for the games and setup," he says. "Let the adults handle the adult things."

"Perfect!" I clap my hands together. "That means there will be lots of time for practice."

"Practice? For what?" Amy asks.

"Our act," I say. "For the talent show. We're a team. We'll do a duet. A song and dance. That Sparkling Crown title is all mine!"

"We aren't singers or dancers," Amy says. "Are you even sure we have the talent? It *is* a *talent* show."

"You don't need to be a great singer or dancer to put on a good show. We can lip-sync. Like stars do during their concerts. We just need a number."

"But you don't have one. Do you?" she asks. Sometimes Amy knows me a little too well.

"Not yet. I'll get another great idea. One as good as the carnival. Then we'll win the talent show and get crowned. Nothing to it. Easy."

"Well, write down that wish list of things you want for the fair," Dad interrupts. "I'll see what the committee can do to make some of it happen."

I shift to reach into my pocket. "Already done." I unfold a piece of paper and toss it onto the passenger seat beside him. It glints a little as it drifts down.

Amy cranes her neck to see it. "You couldn't help yourself, could you?" she asks.

The paper has every line written in a different color. I used my glitter pens. I even made all the letters swirl and curl.

"I could only do so many dull charts. You can't expect me not to sparkle or shine."

Dad pulls into the driveway in front of the condos where Amy lives.

Then he turns to me and says, "No one could ever stop you from doing that, kiddo."

Chapter Three

"Holy crow, Mac," Amy says when she walks into my garage on Saturday morning. "What is going on here?"

I had spent the morning covering the walls in printed pieces of paper with all the ideas I had given my dad. And more. I'd started searching the internet and kept finding new and cool things.

Like a bubble machine. And a lights show. I'd printed them out and stuck them on the wall. Beside each picture, I'd written down the cost and the place to call to order the item.

"What? I did a few Google searches. No big deal."

Amy walks around the garage and reads each printed piece of paper.

She whistles when she's done. "Did you add all this up? There's no way the carnival could break even if the committee ordered all this junk."

"It's not junk. Besides, we can't let my dad make decisions about style." I cross my arms. "You've seen him. He wears socks with sandals. Mom and I have told him not to at least a million times. He doesn't have *vision*. He doesn't know how to dream big."

"Still, this is getting super expensive," Amy says.

I keep my arms crossed. "Cheap. That's what he said. This carnival was my idea. I can't have people saying it was cheap."

"That doesn't mean you have to pick the stuff that costs the most."

I uncross my arms. "I dared to go big. I aimed high. If the committee comes up to my level even a little, it will be fine. I'm willing to budge. I can live without the fireworks show."

"You'll have to," she says. "No way they're going to risk a fire or people getting burned. Plus I think it's actually illegal."

"It was only an idea," I huff.

"A good one," Amy says. "If we had a hundred thousand dollars and all the right connections. Maybe take that one down?"

I nod. "It's pretty though. Look at it." I point at the paper on the wall.

"Really pretty," she agrees.

I sigh. "I wasn't sure they were going to go for the carnival idea. Now that they have, it's like I've got something to prove. It has to be great. It has to make money. People have got to like it. It needs to be *epic*."

Amy goes to take down the fireworks picture. She reaches out and holds a corner of the page. Then she lets it go. "You get that the carnival isn't you. Right? You get that you don't have anything to prove to anyone? You never have. You've been epic ever since we met."

I know she means that to sound good. A small pep talk. Her saying she believes in me and all that. But Amy's always believed in me. She's always been behind my big ideas, no matter how wild. I said let's do a Pride Carnival. She helped figure out how to get the committee to say yes. It's what she does.

Now it's time for everyone else to see me like Amy does. It's my chance for everyone to realize that I, Mac Riley, have fantastic ideas. That I am fantastic. That all the things I am, a diva and a big dreamer, they add up. And what they add up to is a star. Not just any star either. A big, sparkly one. The carnival will bring me one step closer to making everyone understand that. Then there will be no holding me back. No budgets. No price tags. No mean girls making comments. No nothing.

I shiver like someone dropped an ice cube down my back. "I know I'm not the carnival. And, of course, I'm epic. Duh. But I want to be more than epic. What's the word for that?"

Amy shakes her head. "I don't know. It doesn't matter what the word is. You have the coolest ideas. Like trick-or-treating as a duo. We always rake in the candy. Our Mario and Luigi costumes were so good."

"Which is why we're doing the talent show together. We're a pair. A set," I say.

Amy shifts her weight to her other leg. "I wanted to talk to you about that. I'm not crazy about being in the talent show."

"Why? It's not like you get stage fright," I say. "You're fine in front of people."

Amy responds, "I don't know if I want to do it. I don't mind being in the background cheering you on. I'll be there for you. Maybe not right beside you. But there."

"But you're my best friend!" I blurt out. "You have to. You're awesome too!"

Amy laughs. "Oh, I know I'm awesome. I'm really good at letting you have the spotlight. That Sparkling Crown thing is all you. You can do this solo, no problem."

"But we're better together."

Amy shakes her head. "You don't even have an idea for an act."

I laugh. "Like that's going to stop me. I'll get an idea. You'll see. We'll be more than epic. Together. Like it's always been. The act will be like nothing Charles Middle School has ever seen before."

Amy nods. "Well, you really do need me. If for nothing else than to tell you when your ideas may be a little bit too much. Like, is that a horse and carriage?" she asks, looking at a picture on the wall.

"Yes! And we can make it a rainbow horse if we buy the right light. We stick it under the carriage. It will change colors. It's perfect. What else would the Sparkling Crown go around the carnival in?"

"You know that will never get past your dad."

"I know," I say. "But it would look fabulous."

Amy goes back to where she entered the garage. "Okay, walk me through this. Let's get rid of the ideas we know are going to be shot down. Let's give your other ones a real chance. You don't want your dad throwing out all the ideas because of the over-the-top ones. I'll help edit you."

I grin. "I knew you would. Same as I know you'll do the duet. It will turn out better than epic."

Amy doesn't answer.

After we sift through all my ideas, picking out the very best ones, Amy heads back to her home for dinner. That's when it strikes me what the word is for better than epic.

Iconic.

I want to be an icon.

Chapter Four

By Sunday evening I still haven't finished my weekly chores. I have one item left on my list. Vacuuming the living room. I always leave it for last even though it's the easiest job. It takes ten minutes max. Normally.

But normally my mom doesn't have the floor, table and couch covered in open books and stacks of paper. I stand there holding the vacuum.

Her laptop is on the floor in front of her. Her tablet is to her left. Her phone is to her right. She moves from one to another in no real pattern. I can't see a way in. Dad, sitting on the couch, is helping her with invoices.

Mom owns a company that designs and sets up store windows and displays. She even has a huge warehouse filled with cool stuff to create the scenes. There are three Santa's workshops packed away in the warehouse right now, waiting for the holiday shopping season. It's pretty cool walking around in there. Giant spring flowers beside Frosty the Snowman, who is upside down in a pumpkin. Dad says it is probably as close to walking through Mom's brain as we will ever get.

I make a big show of dragging the vacuum hose across the living room. Mom doesn't notice. I shrug and give Dad a look. He shrugs back and returns to his paperwork. There's nothing he can do to make her idea for a display come faster.

I make an over-the-top sighing sound. No response. "Mom?" I ask.

"Mm-hmm?" she mumbles. She doesn't even look up.

"I need to vacuum. It's Sunday."

Mom lifts her head and stares at me. Her eyes take a moment to focus. "Can't you do it later? Or next week?"

Dad pipes up, "He put it off all weekend, Eva. And he skipped last week."

"But I've finally got all my things laid out the way I want. My muse will come. It has to."

"So you're nearly there?" I ask.

Mom shakes her head. "No. I have no idea what I'm going to do. This is for my biggest client. I need to come up with something great. Something…"

"Iconic?" I suggest.

"Yes! Mac gets it!" she says, looking at my dad. "Iconic. That's what I need."

Dad leans forward and kisses the top of her head. "You've got the imagination to do it, hon. You'll get there."

I yank the vacuum, and the hose makes a weird noise. "Well, what about my chores?" I ask.

"Give me a second," Mom says. "I'm sure the right idea will hit me soon. It's out there waiting for me to find it."

"Like me with the talent show." I move some papers on the couch. This is going to take a while. I may as well see what's on TV.

"Please don't sit there. Not there either. And make sure to keep the volume low. I need to concentrate."

I flop onto the chair in the corner. I throw my legs over the arm. Dad tosses me the remote.

I flick from channel to channel. As usual, nothing good is on.

But then I hear a word that makes me stop flicking.

Icon.

I stare at the screen, mesmerized by the image and the captivating narration.

"Singer. Actress. Model. Ally. Comedian. Animal-rights activist. Everything she touches turns to gold. She has won a Grammy, an Emmy and an Oscar. She has over three million followers online and has given more farewell tours than you can count. The Goddess of Pop has defined decade after decade and continues to redefine herself. Cher—The Making of an Icon. *Up next."*

"Turn that up," Mom says.

"That's been on all week," Dad says. "It's one of those biography shows. The part I caught was pretty good. Did you know she rescued an elephant?"

"What? Really?" Mom, an animal lover herself, has been hooked.

"Stop what you're doing and let's watch," Dad says. "I'll grab us some snacks."

We settle in. The documentary starts out with Cher's early performances with her first husband, Sonny Bono. How they rose to fame. How they never quite fit in. How their popularity started to fade and how that affected their marriage.

I was more interested in their style. They really were stunning, especially Cher. Lemon-yellow vinyl. Long black hair past the waist. Striped bell-bottoms. Peace signs. Bright daisies in all colors. The images shown were loud, brave, ahead of their time. Just like Cher was.

And also me.

Mom looks at me during the commercials. We are both wide-eyed. I feel my face slowly pull into a smile. Mom's face does the same. I can feel my smile getting bigger and bigger, until it feels like even my hair is grinning. Her grin is huge too. We sit there like mirrors of one another.

"Icon," Mom says.

"Cher," I answer.

Dad comes back into the living room with a giant bowl of chips. He looks at my mom and then at me.

"Uh-oh," he says. "I've seen those faces before. What kind of trouble are we in?"

Mom and I burst out laughing.

My mom grabs a sketch pad and starts drawing. I get some paper and begin making notes. First, though, I hit the Record button to tape the rest of the Cher program.

"Chips are not going to cut it. I'd better order some pizza," Dad says. He steps over the mess and leaves the room again.

"Hand me those two books?" Mom asks. I grab the ones she points at. "Check this out. I want to show you some of Bob Mackie's work. You want to see an icon? Look at Cher in his gowns. He's dressed all the great divas. Cher. Dolly. Elton John."

I sit on the floor with her and we flip through the pages. The outfits are amazing. They shine. They sparkle. Some look like they're not all there. Some are mostly not there. Each one is a wearable masterpiece.

Dad leans into the doorway. He's got the kitchen phone up to his ear. He smiles at the two of us on the floor. He knows we're onto something. "When an idea hits you two, no one is safe. We're definitely in for some trouble tonight. Oh, hi. I'd like to order a pizza."

"And garlic bread," Mom says. "I'm feeling a *Moonstruck* moment coming on."

Moonstruck is one of Mom's favorite movies, an oldie from the '80s that won Cher an Academy Award. I've never actually seen it, but I'm always up for a cheesy rom-com.

Which reminds me. "With cheese," I say to Dad. "Everything is better with cheese."

He nods. "And two orders of cheesy garlic bread. We're watching *Moonstruck* tonight," he adds. Why he thinks the pizza person will care, I have no idea. "Yup...the one with Cher. No, I *didn't* know a lot of it was filmed in Toronto. That's cool."

Chapter Five

"Don't you want to slap someone now?" Mom asks when the movie is done.

"Yeah, twice! *Snap out of it!*" I say, pretending to slap Mom on the cheek just like Cher did to Nicolas Cage.

"Hey now. Settle down, you two," Dad says.

Mom and I both roll our eyes at him and then

burst into another round of giggles. We've been giggling together most of the night.

Mom pulls her knees up to her chest and wraps her arms around them. "Check these out." In between eating pieces of pizza, we'd both been sketching and making notes as the movie played. "I'm really happy with them." She hands Dad her pad before she stands to stretch.

"They're excellent," he says.

"Thanks!" she says, going into the kitchen to grab a drink. She reappears a moment later. "Okay, *Mermaids* next?"

"What? We're watching another one?" I ask.

"Yes. Cher has appeared to us. Like a vision from heaven. The Goddess of Pop smiled on us. That calls for a double feature. We'll check out *Mermaids* and then maybe some select scenes from her more recent films." She sits back down on the couch.

"I'm game!" I plop down beside her.

"But first, show me what you have been working on."

I hand her my pages of notes and sketches.

"This is solid," Mom says as she flips through. "Really solid. The judges will dig the retro vibe. What were you thinking for costumes?"

I hand my mom another set of pages.

She looks through them. "I think I've got some clothes in storage at the warehouse that could work. I don't think they're Amy's size though. I'm not sure they can be altered for her."

"They wouldn't need to be. That's *my* costume," I tell her.

Dad peeks over Mom's shoulder. "That's a bold move, Mac," he says. "You're sure you want to go there?"

"I need to be bold. I want to win!" I say. "I'm not going to unless I go full out. Cher never played it safe. I won't either. I can't."

Dad pats my shoulder. "You're right. You never have. What do you think about going even bigger? Showier. You need the double slap and snap-out-of-it. Everyone watching needs to feel that hit and want it too."

"Do you mind if I make a few suggestions?" Mom asks. She pulls a pencil out from behind her ear, where she tucked it earlier.

"Go for it," I tell her. I look up at Dad. "And thanks," I say to him. "You have a good point. Let's really wow them."

Dad starts *Mermaids* and then sits down beside me as Mom adds to my sketches. The three of us talk, and my idea comes to life. Mom's tweaks are amazing. And Dad has a better eye for detail than I gave him credit for. I'm sure he will still wear socks with sandals, but I might have to take back some of what I said to Amy about him.

When Cher appears on the screen dressed in her mermaid costume, we all stop and watch.

Mom grabs her sketchbook and begins adding to her designs. Dad pauses the movie so she can study the costume. I point out the little pearls and dangles, the different-colored hairpieces threaded into the wig.

By the end of the second film, my mom and I both have some awesome sketches. They're flashy and daring. They're exactly the looks we were going for. The kind that will be talked about and remembered.

Just like I want to be.

Chapter Six

I spend the next few days working in the garage after school. It's now my carnival home base. But I need to concentrate. I tell Amy not to come over and get my dad to agree not to enter the space until I'm ready.

First I strip the walls of all the internet wish-list items and organize them into a file folder. I use colored tabs. Amy might be the more organized one of us, but I'm the one who knows how to use color. With fresh, clean walls and a lot of tape, I start my work.

My next job requires a bit of stealth. I go inside and hover while my dad makes dinner.

As soon as he puts down his phone to cook, I swipe it. I go over to the charging station and plug it in so that if he catches me, I have a good excuse. I know his passcode, so I scroll through his texts and emails. Nothing interesting about the carnival.

Next I try his office. Jackpot. On a pad by the computer are my dad's notes about the carnival. Who he talked to. Which parents are doing what jobs. I snap photos of the pages and then go back to the garage to finish my setup. Dad will never even know I saw them. I could definitely be a spy. All I need is a black catsuit. I would be the most stylish of spies, of course.

Finally I'm ready. I find Amy as soon as I get to school the next day.

"Can you come over after school?" I ask. "I want to show you what I've done."

"Sure," she says. "I'm excited to hear about your new big idea."

"Great. But I will warn you. Mom is cooking, so it's probably going to be hot dogs for dinner."

Amy laughs. "Your mom's specialty."

I laugh too. "Yeah. She's as busy as ever. But she got the thumbs-up on her designs."

"Good thing we both like hot dogs," Amy says. "I'll text my parents. I'm sure they'll be fine with it. And no one knows how to dress up a hot dog like your mom does."

It's true. Mom likes to grill them. But then she gets creative. She'll add leftover chili, jalapeños and cheese sauce. Once she even threw on some kimchi and made a spicy-and-sour ginger ketchup.

Like her displays show, Mom is an expert on how to dress things up.

Amy's comment reminds me that I should probably give my parents a heads-up that Amy's coming over. I text Dad. He responds right away and tells me to tell Amy that she should stay for dinner. Ha.

Dad picks us up after school. When we get home, I remind him not to come into the garage. "It's part of the surprise." Then I hand him the color-coded file.

"Not a problem. If you need anything, I'll be inside crunching numbers. This is a little more than I was expecting."

"But I took out the fireworks! And the horse and carriages," I say. He has no idea the restraint I've shown.

"Only thanks to me," Amy says.

"Well, thanks for keeping this diva under control," Dad says with a smile. "Have fun, kids."

I punch our code into the panel beside the garage door and say, "Ta-da!" as it lifts.

The walls to my left and right are covered by pieces of poster board. Multicolor, of course. The left wall has become a calendar of tasks and dates. The right, a to-do checklist not just for Amy and me but for every member of the committee. The photos I snapped of Dad's notes really came in handy. With a tiny bit more spy work, I can stay on top of everything going on with my carnival.

The back wall is covered by an old bedsheet I tacked up. I'm saving what's behind it for the big reveal.

Amy's eyes bug out.

"It's fantastic, right?" I ask.

"It looks like a detective's wall from one of those TV crime shows," Amy says. "I thought you had gone extreme before. This is—"

"Next level!" I finish for her. "Those two walls are the boring ones. They're my way of keeping track of the carnival and what was done and what wasn't. You said we had to help."

"I didn't mean you should keep tabs on what *everyone* is doing!" Amy says.

"It's not keeping tabs. It's keeping track. This will make sure everyone stays on task. I don't want anything falling through the cracks. One little thing missed and my dreams for the fair could all fall apart. It's a very fragile balance. I thought you of all people would appreciate my work."

Amy shakes her head. "I don't know if the adults are going to like this. Has your dad seen this?"

"Not yet," I answer.

"He'll want to. Soon." She stares at the bedsheet and frowns. "What's behind the sheet?"

"Our winning routine." I grin as I get the step-ladder.

When the sheet drops, Amy sees the glory. Some people make vision boards. I had to take the entire wall. A Cher wall. And because Cher is a huge deal, I needed an equally huge space. Between the pictures of her in her iconic costumes and outfits there are charts detailing the talent-show number I thought up for Amy and me. Every step noted in order. How they line up with the lyrics. The sketches of our costumes. All my notes. At the top of the wall, as high as I could reach, I've taped a picture of Cher in a gold, beaded halo. It's like she is looking down on us and blessing whatever we do in her name.

"Look down," I tell Amy.

She slowly turns around. The entire cement floor has been taped off in a big red rectangle. I even added Xs and arrows with blue painter's tape to indicate directions.

Before Amy can say anything, I say, "Cher came to me. Well, to us. Mom and me, when we saw this documentary on her. Cher is what's more than epic, exactly what I was looking for. She's iconic.

Decades of hits. Tons of awards. The coolest, most beautiful outfits. She's everything. Cher is life."

Amy looks from the floor to me. "None of this explains what you want to do for the talent show."

"Oops! I jumped ahead," I say. "We do a duet. A classic. Sonny and Cher's 'I Got You Babe.' The judges will love it. It's retro. It's fun. It's cute. My mom said we can borrow costumes. It will be a shining 'flower-power, peace, love and Cher' act. We'll be the stars of the show. That Sparkling Crown is mine!"

"Do you really think kids our age care about Cher?"

"What do you mean? It's Cher! She is a *legend*."

"Maybe. But not everyone is going to know who she is though."

"Well, they should. She's Cher! *Cher!* Her career has been all about staying relevant. That's why she's an icon! Besides, the kids aren't the judges."

Amy sighs. "Okay, so what's the deal with the floor?"

"Those are our moves. I measured the stage. The Xs are where we stand, and the arrows tell us where to go. It's not too complicated—don't worry. Sonny and Cher don't really dance to that song. We still want to look like them performing though." I grab a stack of papers. "I made copies for you. We need to work the whole stage. We should work the crowd too if we can. If they love us, that will sway the judges. Okay, time for practice."

Amy flips through the pages quickly. She shakes her head. "I don't know. I didn't really want to do the talent show to begin with. I told you that."

"Don't worry. I'm doing the heavy lifting," I say, trying to assure her. "You'll be there as support more than anything. Like you wanted. I'll get most of the attention."

"Why's that?" she asks.

I place the tip of my tongue in the center of my lips. Then I pretend to flick my hair back just like Cher used to on the *Sonny & Cher* shows. I've watched all the episodes on YouTube. Mostly the musical performances—I skipped the comedy sketches. Cher was the only funny part of them if they were even funny at all. I deepen my voice a little and make it warble as I say, "Because *I'm* here. I'm Cher."

Chapter Seven

"Back to the top," I say. I march over to the laptop and hit the Stop button.

"Can we take a break?" Amy asks. She leans against my giant checklist.

"Be careful not to smudge the ink on that," I warn. "You're sweaty. We already took a break. We watched all those videos online."

"That wasn't a break. That was you showing me Cher singing 'I Got You Babe' a bunch of times."

"Come on. Let's do it just once more. You're starting to get it. Really. If you give it a little bit more. Try to pretend you are Sonny. When you look at me, it has to be like you know you're the luckiest guy in the world."

"I'm not even a guy!" Amy slides down the wall and sits on the floor. "And you're not even a girl. Are you *sure* you want to do this?"

"Seriously? We've done stuff like this before on Halloween. And you like *RuPaul's Drag Race* as much as I do! It's about expressing yourself. You can be whoever you want. It doesn't matter if you were born a guy or a girl," I say.

"To some people it does. *A lot.*"

"That's their problem," I say. "I can't waste my time arguing with small-minded people like that."

"But they may make it your problem." Amy takes a long drink from the bottle of water I brought out for her. She slides down the wall until she's sitting on the floor. "I don't want to see you get hurt."

"I'll deal with it if it happens," I say. "Now come on. Once more. With feeling."

Amy shakes her head. "But this involves me too. I don't know if I want to *deal* with it."

I slide down the wall beside Amy. I lean against her. "I can take care of myself," I say. "I'm strong enough. I'll take care of you too. Like when we were in kindergarten, remember? You were Thor. And when the older kids tried to steal your helmet I chased them off."

"You charged at them with your light-up unicorn horn," Amy says. "They didn't know what to do with a unicorn running straight at them."

"And I'd do it again, anytime you need me to. Same as you would for me." I hold Amy's fist in my hand and squeeze it.

She bonks my head with hers. "Fine. From the top. But let the record show, I'm still not one

hundred percent on this Sonny and Cher thing."
She stands up and takes her spot.

We go through the song again from start to finish. I think it's better. But there's still a lot of work to do. Amy's Sonny is nowhere close to how good my Cher is. A little sweat. A lot more practice. We'll get there.

We do it twice more. Amy hits her marks, but it seems like the more we practice, the worse she does. She's probably tired.

"How about we call it quits for the night?" I suggest. "Dinner should be ready soon."

Amy nods. She finishes her water and tosses the empty bottle into the recycling bin.

"We can practice every day after school," I say as we enter the house.

"*Every* day?" Amy asks.

"How else will we be ready in time? The Pride Carnival is only two weeks away. Grab a seat. I'll set the table."

Amy plops into a chair at the kitchen table. I grab the dishes. I can see Mom outside on the patio. The grill is smoking. Mom is waving the tongs around as she talks. Dad is seated on the steps.

I slide a cold glass of water over to Amy.

"How did you make the to-do chart?" Amy asks.

I shrug. "Paper. Markers. The usual."

"Yeah, but how did you find out who was doing what?"

I bite the inside of my lip. After a moment I say, "I found a list my dad made."

Amy narrows her eyes. "Why are you being weird about it?"

"Well, he didn't exactly show me. He left a pad out. I happened to see it. It's no big deal," I reply. "And maybe I went through his texts and emails a little. It's not like the information is top secret. It's no big deal."

"Would it be no big deal if he went through *your* phone?" Amy asks.

We both know I wouldn't like that. But I'm not about to admit it. "He's my dad," I say. "It's okay."

"It's *not* okay, Mac. You should have just asked him. And I think you better show him the garage. Fast," she says.

"Sure. Fast," I repeat.

"And stop snooping through all your dad's personal stuff."

"I don't snoop!"

"Right. And Cher doesn't wear wigs," Amy shoots back. "You, Mac Riley, are a great big snoop."

I fake gasp and clutch my chest. I can't help but smile a little bit though. She mentioned Cher. She's making progress. Amy is coming around.

Chapter Eight

"Five, six, seven, eight. Hair flip. Hand on hip. I've got the swagger. You're singing to me. The lip sync has to be bang on. You're half a beat behind." I keep a running commentary as we run through the act again.

We've been doing the number over and over for days. We're not getting any better. Amy is going through the motions. She's always a bit behind.

Either on her lip sync or steps. Or she doesn't move her arms big enough. A few times I caught her rolling her eyes at me.

I let it all go. I figured that was the mature thing to do. Once when she stuck out her tongue at me, I waited until she turned her back before I stuck out my tongue back at her. It doesn't make me less mature if she never saw me, does it?

"We've done this like, a hundred times," Amy huffs. "I know the words. I'm getting tired of practicing this old song."

I resist telling her again that it's not an "old song" but a classic. It was a big hit that defined an era. But I don't. Instead I say, "Practice makes perfect. We can't go onstage without practice. We'll flop. We'll be laughed at. Worse, we'll lose."

"There's a good chance we're going to get laughed at anyway. These costumes are ugly," Amy says.

I stare at the bell-bottom pants Mom brought home for Amy as part of the Sonny costume. They're mustard yellow and fuzzy. I can see her point.

"They're not so bad," I lie. "But we're not done with the costumes yet. We haven't added the rhinestones or flowers or peace signs."

"Those will all go on *your* costume," Amy says.

"You get the furry vest though," I argue. "That's cool, right? Mom is making it out of some fake white yak hair she used for a winter scene a few years ago. It's going to look awesome."

"*Yak?*"

"Fake yak," I say. "And very awesome," I repeat when Amy crosses her arms over her chest.

"We're done for today. I need to get home." Amy picks up her backpack.

I reach out and touch her arm. "Stay for dinner. One more time through."

She shakes her head and hits the button to open the garage door. "My mom was joking at breakfast that she's forgetting what I look like because I'm spending so much time over here. I've got to get home."

I keep my hand on Amy's arm. "How about we try something different," I say.

Amy turns to me. "Seriously?" she asks.

I turn away and then quickly turn back. "You know every single number?" I say dramatically. "You want to show me something? Show me that." I pause then shout, "Wagon Wheel Watusi!"

Amy stares at me.

"You know, from *Burlesque*," I explain. "When Cher demands that Christina Aguilera show her what she can do. So show me something!"

I had made Amy watch that scene at least a half dozen times when we were doing homework. Well, maybe she was actually doing homework. I was watching videos of Cher being iconic.

"Forget it. I need a break," Amy replies. She begins to walk down the driveway.

"Come on. Play along," I say.

"If I played along, I'd be Stanley Tucci," she says. "In fact, I'd rather be eating pasta right now."

"What?" I ask.

"Stanley has an Italian cooking show," Amy explains as she steps onto the sidewalk. "There are other things in the world besides Cher, you know."

Amy is walking way too fast. I have to trot a little to catch up with her.

"I'll walk you home," I offer.

"I'd rather be alone," she says.

I stop at the end of my driveway. "Okay, I guess I'll see you tomorrow?"

Amy stops too. "I know this means a lot to you, Mac," she says. "But I need a break. You've been pushing hard every day."

"I want our act to be special," I say.

"I know. But you're go, go, go. I need a chance to recharge. You probably do too."

"Okay," I reply, because I'm not sure what else to say. I watch her walk down the sidewalk. She does seem tired.

Back in the house, I can hear my dad on the phone in the office. The door is closed.

I hear the words *cancel it* as I creep closer. Is he talking about the carnival?

The floor creaks in the hall, so I can't get closer to listen. But I need to know what's going on. Is everything I worked for going to be for nothing? Something is up.

I know Amy told me no more snooping. But how can I not? I have to find out what's going on. But I can't risk the creaky hall floor and Dad catching me eavesdropping. I could listen in from the phone in the kitchen. But Dad would hear me pick up the other line.

Unless…I could create a diversion. Yes! I have a plan. A good plan. A noisy plan.

I go to the kitchen and pull a bunch of items out of the drying rack by the sink. Two cookie sheets, a pot and lid, three metal bowls and some utensils. I pile everything on top of the cookie sheet. This is the part where I need to work fast.

I let one hand hover above the kitchen phone and the other near the cookie sheet. Then I push the sheet off the counter onto the floor and pull the phone off its hook.

I quickly throw a tea towel over the phone, rush around the counter and plunk myself down on the floor.

I hear the office door open and my dad hurrying down the hall.

"Mac?" he calls out. "Mac? Are you okay? What's going on?"

"I'm okay, Dad!" I call back. "Sorry!" I start to get up as my dad comes into the kitchen.

He steps around the counter and sees me getting to my feet, the cookie sheets, pots and other stuff all over the floor.

"What happened?"

I dust my knees off and rub my butt as if I had landed on it.

"I was putting away the dishes. I piled everything up to do it in one go. I guess it was heavier than I thought," I say.

"You fell?" Dad asks. "Are you hurt?"

I shake my head. "I'm fine. I'll clean it up. Sorry for freaking you out."

Dad looks at the floor. I bend down and start picking things up.

"Make sure you rinse them off. I'm on a call, but I'll only be a couple more minutes," he says. "Be more careful next time," he adds as he walks back down the hall.

When I hear the office door close, I lift the phone receiver to my ear. I keep the tea towel over the mouthpiece.

I hear my dad say, "Thanks for calling to let me know. I'll break the news to Mac."

"I'm sorry," a woman says. Mrs. Khatri. "But we just don't have the money. I know how much Mac wanted all this."

"He dreams big," says my dad. "He's so much like his mom."

"Yes, and he works hard to make those dreams come true," Mrs. Khatri says. "That isn't a bad thing. I'm sorry it didn't work out this time."

"Thanks. For everything…"

They are wrapping up the conversation. I hang up quickly and quietly before I rush to the sink. I yank the tap on. I plunge one of the metal bowls under the flowing water and drop it into the rack.

"Everything okay in here?" Dad asks as he comes back into the kitchen.

"All good," I say.

Except it's not all good. My carnival is in danger.
I have to figure out how to save it.

Chapter Nine

"I'll clear the table," I offer after we finish dinner.

It was my mom's night to cook, but she had called to say she was running late. Dad had defrosted some stew from the freezer. Dinner had been quiet. Both Dad and I were lost in thought. He was probably trying to figure out how to tell me the carnival had been called off. I was trying to figure out how to talk him out of that.

"Try not to drop anything this time," Dad teases as I take his bowl.

"So, Dad," I say as I put our bowls and spoons into the dishwasher, "I wanted to go over a few things about the carnival."

Dad stands up and stretches. "That's good. Because we need to have a talk."

Uh-oh. Anytime anyone says they need to have a talk, it does not end well. It's a rule of life. Having a talk is never a good thing. I take a deep breath as I add a soap cube to the dishwasher.

"There isn't a problem with the carnival, is there?" I ask as if I hadn't overheard him talking earlier. "There haven't been any problems, have there? Like, with Mrs. Khatri?"

Dad leans over the counter and rests on his elbows. "That's a strange way to ask about the carnival. Why would you bring up Mrs. Khatri?"

I shrug. "No reason. Except she's the treasurer. So if money is an issue and the carnival is being canceled, it would make sense that she called earlier."

Dad squints at me over his glasses. "I never told you she called," he says slowly.

I shrug again. A big, slow shrug. I'm trying to buy myself some time, but I know the shrug is too much. Dad must know too. He's still squinting at me as I open my mouth and close it a few times, trying to figure out what to say next.

Dad stands up tall. "Were you listening in on our call, Mac?"

I avoid looking at him. "I might have overheard some things."

"Come clean, Mac. Be honest," Dad says.

I continue not looking at him and don't answer.

"I'm not happy you were listening in on a private conversation. But I guess you heard enough. I'm sorry. I know this isn't how you wanted things to be," Dad says.

"But you can't!" I burst out. "You can't let this

happen! You're the president. You can stop this. There can't be that little in the budget. The carnival has to go on. You can't cancel it!"

"Wait. What? What exactly did you hear?" he asks.

"Everything. *Cancel it. We just don't have the money.* Mrs. Khatri and you being sorry. I don't know how this could happen. How did we go from planning a carnival to not even having one? Mrs. Khatri must have blown all the money somehow. Or stolen it! It can't all be gone," I say. "Maybe that's it! Maybe there's a crime. We need to investigate. We can get it back."

Dad puts a hand on my shoulder. "Calm down."

"I will *not* calm down!" I insist. "Don't tell me to calm down. Not when that thief has ruined my carnival!"

"The carnival is still happening," Dad says.

"Wait. What? But…"

"First, Mrs. Khatri is no thief. She's very smart, and careful with every penny. She's been working hard, and that kind of character assassination is not fair to her," Dad says.

"Sorry," I mumble. "But—"

"No buts. I don't know what you think you heard, but it's clear you didn't hear enough. The carnival is still happening," he says.

"Oh." I feel my shoulders relax a little.

"A big part of that is due to how hard Mrs. Khatri has been working. She had done and redone the budget. She phoned because she was worried you'd take it hard when you found out we can't afford *all* the things you want. Not if we want to keep this as the fundraiser it's meant to be."

"But…" I say, already forgetting about the "no buts" command.

Dad keeps talking. "It's clear she was right. Is that what you have been worrying about? You were tense all through dinner."

I shake my head. "Not just that," I say. I know I need to be completely honest with my dad.

It's time. "I have something for you to see. Amy told me I should have showed you a while ago. Come to the garage."

"I thought you didn't want me to be in your rehearsal space. You said it would ruin the big surprise."

"Come," I say and walk down the hall. I slip on my shoes and open the garage door. I step down first, then flick on the light.

Dad steps down and stops. He looks at the walls. He turns and looks behind him.

"You did all this?" he asks.

I nod.

Dad stands in front of the to-do wall. He crosses the garage to read the task calendar I set for the parents and volunteers.

"You'd make either a really great spy or a really awful one," he finally says.

That's what *I* said! "I wasn't spying," I say out loud. "Or at least I didn't mean to."

"What do you call it?" he asks.

"Amy used the term *snooping*. It sounds nicer. I really couldn't help it. I want this carnival to be good so, so badly. I had to make sure stuff was getting done. I went through your notes to check up on you and the other adults."

"You know that's not okay," he says. We're both quiet for a few moments before he continues, "If this were just about you, like a birthday party or something, I'd be tempted to call it off. You need to learn to respect other people's privacy."

I open my mouth to argue.

Dad holds up a hand. "But this is about the school. The fair brings in a good amount of money. Money that is used by everyone. For books. And supplies. And for kids who can't afford field trips or even proper meals. It's everyone's fair. Not just yours. Hand me that black marker."

I walk to the workbench and pick up the black marker. I put it in my dad's hand.

He goes over to the to-do calendar and pulls it down. He crumples it and throws it into the recycling bin. He moves over to the list of items I wanted for the carnival and who was trying to get them.

"I told you to leave the adults to do the adult jobs," he says as he uncaps the marker. "Here's where we stand." Dad begins to make black *X*s through most of the items on my wish list. The petting zoo. The foam fight. The dry-ice machines.

"Not the light show!" I cry as Dad puts an *X* through it. "That was to replace the fireworks."

"There never were any fireworks," Dad says.

"Only because Amy made me take them out of the mix."

"There were never any fireworks at all, Mac." Dad caps the marker. The list is now almost all black *X*s. "I'm going to be real with you. Your plans were not realistic. We couldn't do most of them.

We tried. We phoned the vendors. We argued over pricing. We tried to get them to go lower. We all loved your ideas and how big and grand they were. You've got something special about you, and it's contagious. People want to be a part of your huge plans and help make them happen. But some dreams take more to achieve than others. Some things are within reach today and some will be in reach in a little bit."

I point to the mostly crossed-out list. "All that's left is an inflatable castle and some face paint. Nothing different from last year."

Dad pats my shoulder. "It won't be the carnival you imagined. But it will be more than a castle and face paint. I promise. I'm going to ask you to do something. I know it's going to be hard for you. You're going to do it anyway."

I twist my mouth to the side and scrunch my lips. I don't nod or agree.

"You're going to focus on your talent-show number. *Only* your talent-show number. That's it. Let the committee take care of the rest."

"But—"

"No. That's it. No more spying. No more going through my notes or checking up on me or the other parents. No more snooping around or listening in. You have to trust me. You're not going to stick your nose in. Or keep us on track. Or monitor our progress. Just focus on your performance."

My dad stands with his hand on my shoulder. He's not squeezing, but I know I can't walk away and ignore him. I know he's waiting for me to agree. I know he knows I don't want to. I can't. I can't give up on the things I want.

But I have to.

"Fine," I say after what feels like forever.

"I'm serious," he says. "I won't cancel the Fun Fair for the whole school. But I can still make *you* stay at home and miss it if I have to."

That hangs between us for a minute. I can't miss my own fair.

So I say, "All right. Only the talent show. That's it."

In my head, though, I'm screaming, *Only the talent show! That's it?*

Dad squeezes my shoulder gently. "Let's go inside. I think I saw some brownies in the freezer. And Mac, the fair may not end up how you wanted. But I can promise it will be better than you think right now."

Before we've even gone back into the house, I've started going through my Sonny and Cher routine in my mind. Every hand move. Every step. Every hair flip. Every sway.

If all I have left is the talent show, I need to bring every wonderful, unbelievable bit of Cher I can to it. It's the only way I can prove to everyone that I am a true icon just like she is.

It's all I have left.

Chapter Ten

I don't see Amy before class or at lunch the next day. I walk around the cafeteria twice with my bag in my hand. Finally I give up and grab the first empty seat I see. I don't know anyone at the table. I eat my lunch quickly and head to the library. She's not there either.

I head outside to the yard. I see Amy on a

bench under the trees. She's got her earbuds in. She's watching something on her phone.

As I get closer, Amy looks up. She pulls out her earbuds.

"What are you doing out here?" I ask.

Amy shrugs. "Fresh air."

I slide onto the bench beside her. I stare at my feet. Amy is swinging one of hers.

"My dad saw the garage," I say.

"That was overdue."

I shrug this time. "I guess you were right about that. And a lot of the other stuff. The carnival won't be happening how I wanted. I had such big plans. Now...nothing."

"It's still happening. I texted your dad last night to see if I could help, in case he needed it. He told me what happened," Amy says.

"Oh."

"I told him he should probably change his

phone password," she says. "And his computer. His email. Maybe get a safe and keep his notepad in it too. So you're not tempted to snoop again."

I roll my eyes. "You're making it sound like so much more than it was. Besides, I was doing it for the greater good of the carnival."

"No. The greater good of Mac Riley," Amy says. It's a little harsh. A lot true. She smiles, though, so I know she's not trying to be mean.

I bump her with my shoulder. "Anyway, I can figure out the new password in no time. All I need to do is clean my dad's phone screen, wait a few hours, then look for fingerprints. It's how I figured it out the first time."

"You really can't help yourself, can you?" Amy says. "But you're going to end up missing the carnival if you do that. Your dad seemed serious."

I huff a little. "I didn't say I *would* do it. I just said I could. There's a difference. I *can* help myself."

"Yeah right," she says. But she's laughing. I'm glad she's not mad at me.

"I thought you might have wanted more time alone when I didn't see you at lunch," I say.

"Maybe a little. I'm ready to get back to practice. But you need to cool it during rehearsals. Things need to be different."

I nod. I open my mouth to tell her how the talent show is the last thing I have left. That now we have to, absolutely have to, win. I stop myself. Instead I throw my arms around her. "You're the best. They will be. Promise. I've already made some changes to the routine. Improvements. It's going to be so much better than before. It has to be."

"I'll see you after school then?" Amy asks.

"That would be great. I'll meet you by your locker. Mom brought home some stuff for us last night. I can't wait for you to see it."

Amy frowns. "What kind of stuff?"

"You'll have to wait and see! After school by your locker. We better get back inside before we're late for class."

Amy and I have separate classes for the afternoon. Time seems to have decided to go slow on purpose. I keep playing "I Got You Babe" on repeat in my head. Sometimes I hum it really low when I think the teacher won't catch me.

After what feels like forever, the final bell rings. I rush to my locker to throw my stuff in before I race to Amy's.

"Are you ready yet?" I ask as soon as I get there.

"No. I only got here a second ago. I need to sort my books." She takes out each book one at a time and stacks them all on the shelf according to size.

"Just throw them in," I say. "You can organize tomorrow!"

Amy continues as if I said nothing. I'm nearly jumping up and down as she calmly organizes her things. Finally she is ready to go.

We head out of the school and jump in my dad's car. I want to tell Dad to floor it. We hit every red light on the way. It's only two traffic signals, but still.

Now that the talent show is all there is left for me to turn into a stunning part of the carnival, I can't wait to get back at it. I'm nearly out of the car even before Dad has finished parking.

"I'll be checking in on you in a bit," Dad says as he heads into the house. "Remember what you agreed to, Mac."

I nod as I open the garage.

"Well. Here we are again," I tell Amy.

She walks into the garage and stares at the walls. She takes a long look at the crossed-out chart and takes in the scraps of the other one, still taped to the wall.

"I guess I should take that down," I say. "I'll do it later. Come see this first." I wave her over to my mom's workbench.

Laid out on top are our costumes. Bell-bottoms. Furry vests. Peace-sign necklaces. Wigs. Everything.

I pick up the yak vest. "Let me help you put it on." I step behind Amy and slide the vest onto her shoulders. "Now grab that wig and mustache." I hold out the furry strip for her to stick on her upper lip.

She doesn't move to take it.

"What's wrong?" I ask.

"That's the first time you've bothered to ask," Amy replies. She takes the fake mustache. "This is wrong." She picks up the wig. "And this. All of this." She tosses the wig and mustache back onto the workbench.

I don't see the problem. "We can trim them and style them. You'll look just like Sonny when we're done with them."

"I see you got this great costume. You're going to look amazing. I'm going to look like I'm wearing a hairy mushroom on my head. And some shag carpet out of someone's basement on my back. Do you not see how I wouldn't want to do that?" She shrugs off the vest and tosses it onto the bench.

I pick up the Sonny wig and shake it out. "The vest makes a statement."

"Yes. And when I've got a hairy lip, the only statement is that I don't care how I look. That I like people laughing at me. Sonny wasn't the good-looking one. He couldn't even sing. If I go on that stage as him, all anyone is going to remember is I'm the dorky, hairy one."

"He got Cher to marry him," I argue. "That says something. We can comb out the vest. It's really not that bad."

"For you," Amy says. "Because you get to be the beautiful one."

"Because I'm Cher!" I exclaim. "I'm the taller one of us. I'm the one who has the moves. I'm the clear star! Besides, you said you didn't care about the talent show or winning. You were happy to fade into the background and let me shine."

"None of that means I want to get made fun of. It doesn't mean I want to be the boring half of the duo," Amy says.

"The carnival is next week. It's already a total disaster. Our talent-show act can't be one too. I don't know why you waited until now to tell me all this."

"I tried to tell you from the start," Amy says. "No matter how many times I brought it up, you didn't want to hear it. You decided not to listen. I've been telling you all along. I don't want to be the boring old dead guy!"

I do the Cher tongue thing again. "It's really not that bad."

Amy scowls at me. She grabs the long black Cher wig. "Fine. If it isn't so bad, why don't I be Cher? You be Sonny."

My jaw drops. "You are *not* Cher," I say.

"Why can't I be? Why can't I be the cool one? The talented one. The alive one at least. Why?" she asks.

"Because you're not iconic!" I yell. "*I* am. Me! I thought up the carnival. I thought up the routine. I am the big dreamer. I'm Cher! Not you!"

Amy throws the wig onto the workbench and picks up her bag. "Yeah, well, I'm not Sonny."

I don't say anything.

Amy walks out of the garage. She stops and turns back.

"You might be the one with the big ideas. But I'm not some prop to Mac Riley, wannabe Cher. You still aren't listening. You don't think of me as anything more than some part of your act. The same way people thought of Sonny next to Cher. If you're such an icon, do it alone. Do the song by yourself." She turns and walks away.

"I will!" I yell. "Cher didn't need Sonny! I don't either!"

Chapter Eleven

I slam the door as I enter the house.

"Careful now," Dad calls from the kitchen. "Is Amy staying for dinner? I made you kids some snacks."

"Amy bailed," I say. I yank out a kitchen chair and throw myself onto it.

Dad frowns. "Explain," he says.

"She went home. She's not doing the routine. She won't be Sonny. She said she never wanted to. She told me to be Sonny. *Me!* Sonny! Yeah right! I'm a Cher if there ever was one. You can't make a Cher into a Sonny."

Dad leans on the counter. "I know you're upset—"

"I'm angry. Furious. She left. What am I supposed to do now? I have to redo the entire routine," I say.

"But," Dad continues, "maybe she had reasons. You two have been friends a long time."

"She didn't think about that when she walked out on me."

Dad shakes his head. "I'm going to let you be angry. When you calm down, you should figure out what you're going to do about Amy. You've been friends for too long to fall out over a small fight. Especially when the fight is about Sonny and Cher."

Dad walks around the counter and puts a plate

of crackers and dip in front of me. Half the crackers are the kind I like. The other half are the kind Amy likes. I shove the plate away and stomp back to the garage. I've got a new act to figure out.

I'm dancing solo and trying to do the routine alone.

It's fine. It doesn't totally suck. But I know it doesn't really work either. It's a duet. It's missing something without Amy. Even when she was half a beat behind.

But Amy's not here, and I need a Sonny for the song. The school doesn't have a screen big enough for me to sing with a video of Sonny like Cher did at her concerts. The best I could do would be to put a laptop on a stool beside me to lip-sync with. That would look sad and small. Not impressive. Not iconic.

I listen to Cher's other songs. There's a long

list of hits. But to look really good onstage, I'd need great lighting. Or huge props. Or a battleship. Or to get lowered from the ceiling while wearing a huge white fur coat and hat. I have none of those. And there's no time to get them.

I stare at the chart with all the Xs on the garage wall. I walk over and rip it down, crumple it into a ball and shove it into the recycling bin.

I slam the garage door every time I come back into the house. Dad doesn't say anything.

But after days of me slamming doors and trying out new routines and failing miserably, Mom comes out to the garage.

"We should do a fitting for your costume," she says. She pulls a chair on wheels over to the workbench and sits down.

"What for?" I ask. "I thought I didn't need Amy anymore. But I can't do a song meant for two by myself. And I can't figure out a new number. I should drop out of the show."

Mom pulls a number of items from her sewing kit—pins, needles, chalk, measuring tape and thread. "It's not easy," she says.

"What isn't?"

"Being you and me. I get these huge ideas too. I want things a certain way. I can be hard. Demanding. I want my plan A. Sometimes that pays off. But only sometimes," she says.

"And the rest of the time?"

"The rest of the time I end up making things harder than they have to be. I don't listen. I insist on everyone doing it my way. I don't take help." Mom shakes her head. "Then I remind myself that the important people in my life want me to succeed. They try to support me. To help me. They're not trying to tell me my plans suck. Or standing in my way. Sometimes I need to check myself so I don't hurt the people who are always by my side." She tosses me the bell-bottoms with the sparkly flowers on them. "Try on the pants. I can take them in if they're too big."

I duck behind the recycling bin and slip on the pants.

When I come out, Mom says, "They fit like they were made for you."

"Except I probably won't get a chance to wear them. There are no other options. I have to drop out," I say.

Mom starts packing up her sewing kit. "That doesn't need to be your plan B."

She pulls something out of the kit. She stands and tacks it onto my "icon" wall, right below Cher in the halo. Then she heads back into the house.

I walk over to the wall and study what she has pinned there. It's a picture of Amy and me when we were little. Amy is dressed as a Thor, and I'm a unicorn. We have our arms across each other's shoulders and grins a mile wide.

Chapter Twelve

At the end of the week, I ask Dad to stop at Amy's building on the way home. I was hoping to speak to her at school, but I never found her. I've decided to wait for her at her condo.

Dad pulls into the driveway. "Do you want me to stay?"

I shake my head. "I'll be okay walking home. I need to fix things with her. You told me that a few days ago. It was good advice. I should have taken it sooner."

"See you soon then," Dad says.

I pace in front of the glass doors to Amy's lobby. When I spot her walking toward the building, I duck behind one of two potted pine trees near the entrance. I don't want her to avoid me by taking the side entrance. There's something I need to say to her.

Amy stops in front of the other pot when she sees me.

We stare at each other. My mouth goes dry. I swallow. It feels like I have sand in my mouth.

"I came to say sorry," I blurt out. I can't let my sand mouth stop me. "You were right. I didn't listen. I made you the boring one. I didn't care. And you tried to help me. With the carnival. With the song you didn't want to do. With everything. Like you always do."

Amy doesn't answer, so I keep talking. "I'm dropping out of the talent show. The duet stinks with only one person. I can't do it without you. I don't want to," I ramble. "And you *are* a Cher. You're the real Cher. I dream. But you do. I don't know why I said those things I said. I was wrong. I'm sorry."

Amy adjusts her backpack. "The song didn't stink. It was good. I just didn't want to wear a mustache and that awful wig. I wanted to be as great as you. I think I wanted to be a diva too."

"I didn't think about how you felt," I admit. "I wanted things my way."

Amy nods. "I accept your apology. You're still wrong though."

"I know," I say. "I really am sorry. If I could turn back time…"

Amy rolls her eyes. "Do you really think more Cher lyrics are going to help? You're not listening, again. I mean you're wrong to drop out of the talent show. The number is good. But it needs to be good for both of us. If you still want to do it together, I have some ideas. I don't know how much you want that solo career."

"All I really want to do is be friends with you. I'm ready to listen." I add, "Properly."

Amy reaches for the lobby door. "It's going to be a lot of work to pull it off. But Cher seems like a hard worker."

"She's got to be. She's still going after over half a century," I say.

"Call your dad. Tell him you're eating dinner here."

We walk into the lobby side by side. I feel like doing a strut across it, but I hold back.

"Mac?" Amy says as we wait for the elevators.

"Yes?" I answer.

"I'm going to need you to do the Wagon Wheel Watusi."

I must look shocked, because Amy starts laughing.

"Snap out of it," she says, pretending to slap my face.

We're both laughing when the elevator arrives.

Chapter Thirteen

"Five, six, seven, eight," Amy counts us in. "Pick it up, Mac. Bigger hand motions. This is Cher. Do her justice. Flip that hair!"

Right on beat Mom struts into the garage, slinging a glue gun. She sits down at the workbench. It's covered in dog chew toys. The kind that squeak. Pork chops and T-bone steaks from a display she did last year for a pet-store chain.

"You're sure the new costumes will be done for tomorrow night?" Amy asks her.

"I'm a woman with a glue gun," Mom answers. "I can do anything. You kids keep going through your new routine. I've got this. By the way, where did you find this mix?"

"YouTube! First rule of the internet. If you can think of it, it's probably already there," Amy says. "I can't believe the carnival is tomorrow."

"You've given this your all these last couple of days," Mom says. "If you two don't win..."

"Then we had fun," I say. "Together."

Amy gives me a thumbs-up and counts us in again.

After Mom finishes the costumes and drives Amy home, I offer to help Dad sort the prizes for the game booths.

"Bed," Mom says firmly when she returns. "You

need your rest. I'll help your dad. And I've taken tomorrow off too."

Dad looks up from his clipboard. He's been checking off items to be loaded into the car. "But I thought you had that big client," he says.

"I've got a good team working on it. They can handle things. I can take one day to help my husband and kid," she says. "Up to bed, Mac." She stands beside my dad. "Tell me what you need me to do. Consider it done."

I dance up the stairs. It's all coming together. Tomorrow is going to be so awesome!

Chapter Fourteen

The Pride Carnival looks so much better than I thought it would. The booths are decorated in different colors. People are walking around with their faces painted. They eat hot dogs and popcorn and ice cream and cotton candy.

The inflatable bouncy castle and slide light up from the inside. There is a dunk tank. The track is being used for a three-legged race. People soaked and laughing stagger out of the water-gun area. Food trucks have pulled into the yard all along one fence. There's two high school guys named Benji and Theo who have volunteered at our school before. They are running a bake-sale stand. The lineup is huge. People are shoving cupcakes in their mouths before they even walk away from the stand.

As the sun sets, the sky turns hot pink and orange before it fades into blues and purples. Almost like we planned a rainbow sky! The moon is full and beautiful. The stars wink on.

Dad pulls me aside. "Watch this," he says as he points up. Strings of lights twinkle on over the entire schoolyard. Every color of the rainbow sparkles and blinks. The crowds walking through the carnival change from red to yellow to blue to green.

"I thought we couldn't afford anything like this. What about the budget?" I ask.

"All the parents brought their holiday lights. I told your mom what I wanted, and the two of us figured out how to do it. We're a good team. We wanted something special for you."

I throw my arms around my dad and hug him.

Different kinds of lights start flashing from the street. I look over and see two police cars and a fire engine pulling up to the curb. I look from them to my dad. Did we break some kind of rule?

He laughs. "Don't worry. I asked if they'd come. Everything is going as planned. Now go get into your costume. The talent show starts soon."

I run through the crowd of people. The air is filled with laughter and the smell of funnel cake and corn dogs. People are talking loudly, calling to their friends. And the rainbow lights! It's nothing like I thought it would be. But in so many ways it's much better.

Mrs. Khatri is monitoring the doors to the school, letting people in one by one to use the washrooms.

She stops me on my way in. "This was a great idea, Mac," she says. "Exactly what the Fun Fair and the school needed. Thank you."

"No, thank *you*," I say. "It's so much better than I thought it would be. I mean that." I duck inside to transform in the gym changerooms.

When I come back out, I keep my head down. I don't want anyone to recognize me in my costume. The long dark hair of the wig hides my face. I hurry behind the stage area. Amy is already there.

"We're on last," she says. "Only a couple more acts."

I nod. In my head I'm going through the steps. I feel a little sweaty, and the smell of all the fried foods is making me feel kind of sick. I wonder if Cher ever feels nervous before going onstage. I stand tall and order my stomach to settle down. I am Cher, and I can do this.

We stand quietly and watch the other acts.

When the guy who yodels leaves the stage, I take my place.

Amy gives me a thumbs-up from where she's waiting in the wings. I hear the music, and right on cue, I step out. Hair flip. Cher tongue. Lip-sync. The flowers on my bell-bottoms shine. My peace-sign necklace twinkles.

The judges smile. The crowd cheers. I sway with the music. Then Amy steps out from her side of the stage. *Her* bell-bottoms swish. The furry vest looks so good under the lights picking up all the colors in the fake fur. The mustache and wig are still kind of dorky-looking. Amy was right. But she looks like Sonny. I break out into a smile when we hit the chorus. The crowd sways with us to the music and "Babe" with us.

As the song ends, I rush offstage holding hands with Amy. I rip off the bell-bottoms and my top. She helps me into a black leather jacket to go over the bodysuit I am wearing under my first costume. Mom glue-gunned belts across the bodysuit, and I have on boots that go above my knees. I pull a new wig on. Amy adjusts it.

"You're on. I'll change and be out there in a second," she says. She gives me a push onto the stage so I don't miss my cue.

I raise my head and see the lights. The carnival glitters around me. I skip out onto the stage. My black curly wig bounces around me. I lip-sync to the beginning of "If I Could Turn Back Time" as the crowd cheers. A sailor's cap flies out from the wings just the way Amy and I planned. I skip over to pick it up and put it on my head.

Then the music changes and begins to pump. *Rah rah rah rah rah. Ro ma ro ma ma.*

Amy struts from the wings, hands on hips, pausing to pose. Her dress and platform boots are covered with the fake-steak dog chew toys. Mom did a great job of recreating the famous outfit

Lady Gaga wore to an awards show. Amy has mirrored sunglasses that wrap around her face and look like they spark with the flashes of the lights. Right on cue, she lip-syncs the first verse of "Bad Romance."

Suddenly we hear sirens hoot. The lights from the police cars and fire engine start blinking on and off like strobes. The songs change up and mix together. I bounce forward and bop along with Amy to the "If I Could Turn Back a Bad Romance" mashup. Except it's not us. I swear, in that moment it's Cher and Lady Gaga onstage. We *are* them. Sure, it's our bodies and costumes. But it feels like we're them. It feels…iconic. We are two divas sharing a stage. We are legends.

Chapter Fifteen

Amy and I hug each other and bounce up and down as soon as we're offstage.

"That was the great thing! That was more than epic!" Amy screams over the cheering crowd.

"It was all your idea."

"It was *our* idea," Amy corrects. "Don't you forget it."

"Not for a second," I scream back.

Mom rushes over to us. "Your dad needs you now," she yells. "Hurry. Let's go."

"Is everything okay?" I ask.

"Everything's fabulous," she says. "Hurry."

We rush through the crowds. Mom holds my hand. I hold Amy's. We snake and weave through all the people, over to the curb where the police cars are.

A news truck is there. Dad has a camera pointed at him. A woman in a suit holds a microphone held in front of his face.

"I might have made a few calls when the crowd got so huge," Mom says.

"We didn't expect this sort of turnout," my dad says into the mic. "The community support tonight has been unbelievable. More people came out than we've ever had before."

"This was your son's idea?" the suited reporter asks. "Where is he?"

Dad looks around for me.

Mom shoves me forward.

I know exactly what to do. I hold tight to Amy's hand as I step forward. I wait until I know we're on camera before I do the Cher tongue move and hair flip.

"It was *our* idea," I say. "My best friend, Amy Chen, helped me every step of the way. And all the parents on the Fun Fair committee worked so hard to make tonight happen."

Mrs. Khatri comes racing up to us. "Mac! Amy! The votes are in. You won the talent show. Your act has been named the Sparkling Crown of the Carnival."

She hands me a tiara and sash. I can't help but admire all the glitter and sequins on both. I know my mom's work when I see it. She's a powerful woman with a glue gun.

"Would you mind us filming you putting that on for the interview?" the reporter asks me.

I reach up and adjust my sailor's cap. "I've got my crown for the evening. Amy needs hers."

I give a big smile to the camera as I remove the rubber steak pinned into Amy's wig and place the tiara on her head.

"How did you two think of changing the Fun Fair into the big success going on behind you?" the reporter asks.

"It was all Mac," Amy says.

"I came up with the idea of a Pride Carnival theme. But Amy knew it would be good for our community and she kept me from going overboard," I say. "I definitely need that."

"Mac knows how to dream big," Amy says, leaning into the mic.

I turn to her. "And you know how to make sure my dreams don't get so big they explode and make a mess everywhere," I say. "I'm so lucky I've got you."

Amy grins.

I grin back.

We both know what comes next.

At the exact same time, we both say, "Babe!"

Acknowledgments

My thanks to Orca Books for being the right home for stories like this one and to my iconic editor, Tanya, the Amy who makes big dreams into realities. It was Tanya who had the brilliant vision to put Gaga and Cher in a scene together and led me to discover their unreleased track. There are no thanks large enough.

As always, thank you to my family and friends, especially Matthew and Amanda, who let me borrow from their lives a tiny bit. That definitely sounds classier than "I took something they did and wrote it down."

My friend Melanie Florence, you have my thanks for always being excited with me no matter how many Cher texts and videos I send you. Warning: It's only going to get worse.

And of course, my thanks to the Canadian kidlit community and CANSCAIP for all you do to support us and our books.

I'm so grateful I've got you, babes.

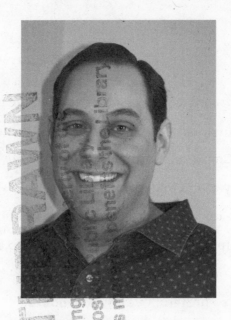

Paul Coccia is the author of the bestselling Orca Soundings title *Cub*, which was a Junior Library Guild Gold Standard Selection, and *The Player*. His most recent book, *On The Line*, was co-authored with Eric Walters. Paul has an MFA in creative writing from the University of British Columbia and lives in Toronto with his family.